For Wally

First U.S. small hardcover edition 2002

The Library of Congress has cataloged the large hardcover second edition as follows:

Handford, Martin.
Where's Waldo? / Martin Handford. —2nd U.S. ed.
p.   cm.
Summary: The reader follows Waldo as he hikes around the world and must
try to find him in illustrations of some of the crowded places he visits.
ISBN 0-7636-0310-4 (large hardcover)
[1. Voyages and travels—Fiction. 2. Humorous stories. 3. Picture puzzles.] I. Title.
PZ7.H1918 Wh   1997
[Fic]—dc21   97-014990
ISBN 0-7636-1920-5 (small hardcover)

6 8 10 9 7

Printed in China

This book was typeset in Wallyfont.
The illustrations were done in watercolor and water-based ink.

Candlewick Press
2067 Massachusetts Avenue
Cambridge, Massachusetts 02140

visit us at www.candlewick.com

MARTIN HANDFORD

CANDLEWICK PRESS
CAMBRIDGE, MASSACHUSETTS

HI, FRIENDS!

MY NAME IS WALDO. I'M JUST SETTING OFF ON A WORLDWIDE HIKE. YOU CAN COME TOO. ALL YOU HAVE TO DO IS FIND ME.

I'VE GOT ALL I NEED — WALKING STICK, KETTLE, MALLET, CUP, BACKPACK, SLEEPING BAG, BINOCULARS, CAMERA, SNORKEL, BELT, BAG, AND SHOVEL.

BY THE WAY, I'M NOT TRAVELING ON MY OWN. WHEREVER I GO, THERE ARE LOTS OF OTHER CHARACTERS FOR YOU TO SPOT. FIRST FIND WOOF (BUT ALL YOU CAN SEE IS HIS TAIL), WENDA, WIZARD WHITEBEARD, AND ODLAW. THERE ARE ALSO 25 WALDO-WATCHERS SOMEWHERE, EACH OF WHOM APPEARS ONLY ONCE IN MY TRAVELS. CAN YOU FIND ONE OTHER CHARACTER WHO APPEARS IN EVERY SCENE? ALSO IN EVERY SCENE, CAN YOU SPOT MY KEY, WOOF'S BONE, WENDA'S CAMERA, WIZARD WHITEBEARD'S SCROLL, AND ODLAW'S BINOCULARS?

WOW! WHAT A SEARCH!

Waldo

YODEL-ODEL-EE,
WALDO'S GANG!
I WALKED ACROSS THE SKI
SLOPES TODAY AND SAW
SOME INCREDIBLE SIGHTS!
THERE WAS THIS SKIER
GIVING FLOWERS TO HIS
GIRLFRIEND, AND ANOTHER
WITH AN ANCHOR OVER HIS
SHOULDER, AND ONE ALL
ROLLED UP IN A SNOWBALL!
WOW! INCREDIBLE!

Waldo

TO:
WALDO'S GANG
UPSTAIRS,
DOWNSTAIRS,
ALL OVER THE
PLACE

HUFF PUFF WALDO-SPOTTERS!
I LOVE TRAIN STATIONS,
DON'T YOU? THERE WAS SO
MUCH GOING ON TODAY—
COWS ESCAPING FROM TRUCKS,
A MAN ASLEEP BETWEEN THE
TRACKS, DOGS CAUSING ALL
SORTS OF TROUBLE!
IT WAS REALLY WILD!

Waldo

TO:
WALDO-SPOTTERS
ACROSS THE SEA,
DOWN THE ROAD,
AROUND THE BEND

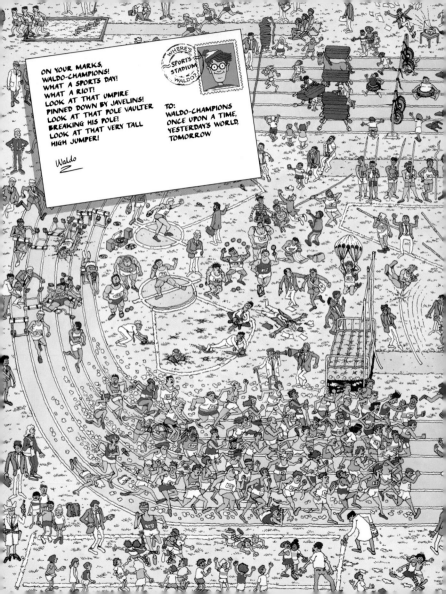

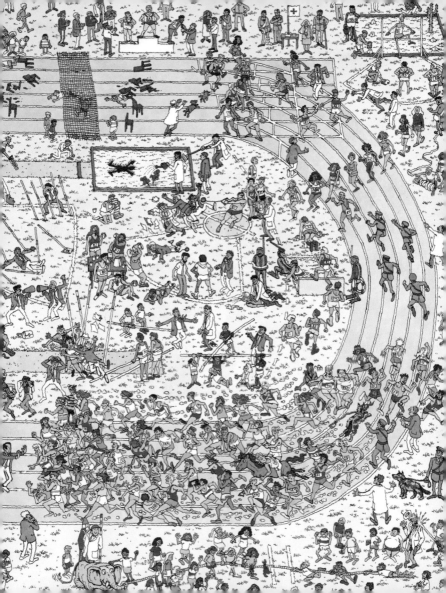

HOW-DE-DOO, WALDO-SCHOLARS!
I'M SMART, AS YOU KNOW.
I GO TO MUSEUMS TO LEARN
THINGS. TODAY I FOUND OUT
ABOUT TICKLING THE TOES OF
A MAN IN THE STOCKS; ABOUT
KNOCKING DOWN A SUIT OF
ARMOR; ABOUT THE
EGYPTIAN MUMMY'S BABY.
NOW, THAT'S LEARNING!

Waldo

WHERE'S
≈ MUSEUM
WALDO?

TO:
WALDO-SCHOLARS
AT SCHOOL,
IN TROUBLE,
AGAIN

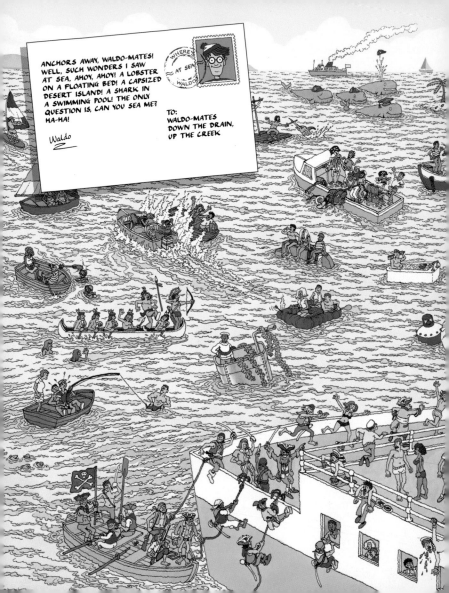

ANCHORS AWAY, WALDO-MATES!
WELL, SUCH WONDERS I SAW
AT SEA, AHOY, AHOY! A LOBSTER
ON A FLOATING BED! A CAPSIZED
DESERT ISLAND! A SHARK IN
A SWIMMING POOL! THE ONLY
QUESTION IS, CAN YOU SEA ME?
HA-HA!

Waldo

TO:
WALDO-MATES
DOWN THE DRAIN,
UP THE CREEK

WATCH IT, WALDO-HUNTERS!
I'M AN ANIMAL LOVER, THAT'S
FOR SURE. I LOVE THAT HIPPO
WITH ITS ALARM CLOCK; THAT
LION HAVING ITS MANE COMBED;
THAT HAT-EATING GIRAFFE;
THOSE OWLS IN SUNGLASSES.
GREAT!

Waldo

WHERE'S
SAFARI PARK
WALDO?

TO:
WALDO-HUNTERS
NICE PLACE,
THE JUNGLE,
OUTSIDE

HEY, WALDO-WATCHERS!
SAW SOME TRULY TERRIFIC
SIGHTS TODAY — SOMEONE
BURNING TROUSERS WITH
AN IRON; A LONG THIN MAN
WITH A LONG THIN TIE;
A GLOVE ATTACKING A MAN.
PHEW! INCREDIBLE!

Waldo

TO:
WALDO-WATCHERS
OVER THE MOON,
THE WILD WEST,
NOW

WHERE DEPARTMENT STORE WALDO?

STEP RIGHT UP,
WALDO-FUN-LOVERS!
WOW! I'VE LOST ALL MY
THINGS, ONE IN EVERY PLACE.
NOW YOU HAVE TO GO BACK
AND FIND THEM. AND SOME-
WHERE ONE OF THE WALDO-
WATCHERS HAS LOST THE
BOBBLE FROM HIS HAT. CAN
YOU SPOT WHICH ONE AND
FIND THE MISSING BOBBLE?

Waldo

TO:
WALDO-FUN-LOVERS
BACK TO THE BEGINNING,
START AGAIN,
TERRIFIC

THE GREAT WHERE'S WALDO? CHECKLIST

Hundreds more things for Waldo-watchers to watch out for!

IN TOWN

- A dog on a roof
- A man on a fountain
- A man about to trip over a dog's leash
- A car crash
- A happy barber
- People in a street, watching TV
- A puncture caused by a Roman arrow
- A tearful tune
- A boy attacked by a plant
- A waiter who isn't concentrating
- A robber who's been clobbered
- A face on a wall
- A man coming out of a manhole
- A man feeding pigeons
- A bicycle crash

THE TRAIN STATION

- A boy falling from a train
- A breakdown on tracks
- Naughty children on a train roof
- People being knocked over by a door
- A man about to step on a ball
- Three different times at the same time
- A wheelbarrow baby carriage
- A face on a train
- Five people reading one newspaper
- A struggling bag carrier
- A showoff with suitcases
- A man losing everything from his cases
- A smoking train
- A squeeze on a bench
- A dog tearing a man's trousers
- Fare dodgers
- A hand caught between doors
- A cattle stampede
- A man breaking a weighing machine

SKI SLOPES

- A man reading on a roof
- A flying skier
- A runaway skier
- A backward skier
- A portrait in snow
- An illegal fisherman
- A snowball in the neck
- Two unconscious skiers
- Two skiers hitting trees
- An Alpine horn
- A snow skier
- A flag collector
- Two very scruffy skiers
- A skier up a tree
- A water-skier on snow
- An abominable snowman
- A skiing reindeer
- A roof jumper
- A heap of skaters

ON THE BEACH

- A dog biting a boy's bottom
- A man who is overdressed
- A muscular man with a medal
- A popular girl
- A water-skier on water
- A striped photo
- A punctured air mattress
- A donkey who likes ice cream
- A man being squashed
- A punctured beach ball
- A human pyramid
- A human steppingstone
- Two odd friends
- A cowboy
- A human donkey
- Age and beauty
- A boy who follows in his father's footsteps
- Two men with vests, one without
- A boy being tortured by a spider
- A showoff with sandcastles
- A gang of hat robbers
- An Arab making pyramids
- Three protruding tongues
- Two oddly fitting hats
- An odd couple
- Five spiders
- A towel with a hole in it
- A punctured pontoon boat
- A boy who's not allowed any ice cream

CAMPSITE

- A bull in a hedge
- Bull horns
- A shark in a canal
- A bull seeing red
- A careless kick
- Tea in a lap
- A low bridge
- People knocked over by a mallet
- A man surprised undressing
- A bicycle tire about to be punctured
- Camper's camels
- A scarecrow that doesn't work
- A wigwam
- Large biceps
- A collapsed tent
- A smoking barbecue
- A fisherman catching old boots
- An old-fashioned bicycle
- Boy Scouts making fire
- A roller-skating hiker
- A man blowing up a boat
- A camper's butler
- Runners on a road
- A bull chasing children
- Scruffy campers
- Thirsty walkers

SPORTS STADIUM

- Three pairs of feet, sticking out of sand
- A cowboy starting races
- Hopeless hurdlers
- Ten children with fifteen legs
- A record thrower
- A shot put juggler
- An ear trumpet
- A vaulting horse
- A runner with two wheels
- A parachuting vaulter
- A Scotsman with a caber
- An elephant pulling a rope
- People being knocked over by a hammer
- A gardener
- Three frogmen
- A runner without any shorts on
- A bed
- A bandaged boy
- A runner with four legs
- A sunken jumper
- A man with an odd pair of legs
- A man chasing a dog, chasing a cat
- A boy squirting water